Dear Parent:
Your child's love of reading starts here!

Every child learns to read in a different way and at his or her own speed. Some go back and forth between reading levels and read favorite books again and again. Others read through each level in order. You can help your young reader improve and become more confident by encouraging his or her own interests and abilities. From books your child reads with you to the first books he or she reads alone, there are I Can Read Books for every stage of reading:

SHARED READING
Basic language, word repetition, and whimsical illustrations, ideal for sharing with your emergent reader

BEGINNING READING
Short sentences, familiar words, and simple concepts for children eager to read on their own

READING WITH HELP
Engaging stories, longer sentences, and language play for developing readers

READING ALONE
Complex plots, challenging vocabulary, and high-interest topics for the independent reader

I Can Read Books have introduced children to the joy of reading since 1957. Featuring award-winning authors and illustrators and a fabulous cast of beloved characters, I Can Read Books set the standard for beginning readers.

A lifetime of discovery begins with the magical words **"I Can Read!"**

Visit www.icanread.com for information
on enriching your child's reading experience.

Pinkalicious®
Fishtastic!

To Carly and Jaden
—V.K.

The author gratefully acknowledges
the artistic and editorial contributions of
Daniel Griffo and Jacqueline Resnick.

I Can Read® and I Can Read Book® are trademarks of HarperCollins Publishers.

Pinkalicious: Fishtastic!
Copyright © 2019 by Victoria Kann

PINKALICIOUS and all related logos and characters are trademarks of Victoria Kann. Used with permission.

Library of Congress Control Number: 2018958440
ISBN 978-0-06-284039-4 (trade bdg.) — ISBN 978-0-06-284038-7 (pbk.)

19 20 21 22 23 SCP 10 9 8 7 6 5 4 3 2 1
❖
First Edition

I Can Read!

BEGINNING 1 READING

Pinkalicious®
Fishtastic!

by Victoria Kann

HARPER
An Imprint of HarperCollins*Publishers*

I felt a tug on my line.

Peter and I were fishing.

"I caught something!" I cheered.

I reeled in my line.

"Get ready," I told Peter.

"Here comes the prettiest,

pinkest fish in the—"

I stopped short.

Something was on my line,
but it wasn't pretty,
and it wasn't a fish.
"HA HA HA!" Peter laughed.
"You caught an old boot!"

"Where are the fish?" I asked.

Then I felt a tug.

"This is it," I said.

"My pinkatastic catch!"

I reeled in . . .

a shell.

Suddenly Peter's rod wiggled.

"I got something!" he said.

Peter pulled out a big fish.

It had big eyes, crooked teeth,

and sharp fins.

"Wow!" Peter said.

"What an odd fish!"

He held the fish up to my face.

"I caught the best fish ever,"

Peter said.

I jumped away.

"Ewwww!" I said.

"More like the ugliest fish ever."

"At least I caught a fish,"
Peter bragged.

"That is not a fish," I said.

"It's a . . . a . . . MONSTER!"

"A monster fish!" Peter said.

"Cool!"

He put the fish

in a bucket of water.

"I'm going to take him home

as a pet," he said.

We peeked inside the bucket.

The monster fish's mouth was open.

"I think he's hungry," Peter said.

He dumped the rest of our bait

into the bucket.

"Hey!" I yelled.

"How am I going to catch
a pinkatastic fish without bait?"

"Oops," said Peter.

Peter went to get more bait.

I was alone with the monster fish.

"Yuck," I said.

The monster fish looked up.

His eyes met mine.

They were huge.

They also looked a little sad.

I looked at the big ocean.

I looked at the small bucket.

"You don't like it

in that tiny bucket, do you?"

I asked the fish.

The fish bumped into the side

of the bucket.

He made a splash with his tail.

"Poor fishy," I said.

"I bet you want to go home."

"I'll help you," I said.

I put the monster fish

back into the ocean.

Peter came running over.

"My monster fish!" he yelled.

"What happened?"

Before I could respond,

we heard a loud splash.

The monster fish was diving
through the waves!

"He looks happy now," I said.

"I guess he does," Peter said.

Suddenly the fish blew some bubbles.

It made a beautiful noise.

"It sounds like singing!"

I said.

The bubbly water droplets
made an amazing melody.
Whiiish, whoooosh, fizzzzz!
Tink, tink, ting!
The tune was so pretty,
we couldn't help but hum along.

A dolphin and a school
of pink fish swam over.
So did a family of sea stars.
"They love his song as much
as we do!" said Peter.

More fish gathered to listen.

They flapped and splashed

their fins to the music.

I watched the monster fish.

He didn't look so ugly anymore.

I barely noticed his sharp fins
or his big eyes.

"Your fish isn't beautiful because
of how he looks!" I told Peter.

"He's beautiful because
of how he sounds!"

The monster fish spewed
a fountain of water
and sang a final note.
Then he jumped out of the ocean—
straight toward me!

The monster fish gave me

a big, wet kiss.

I laughed.

"You're quite welcome," I said.

"You might not be pinkapretty,"

I told the fish.

"But you are magni-fish-cent!"